# One Snowy Morning

**Kevin Tseng**

*illustrated by* **Dana Wulfekotte**

DIAL BOOKS FOR YOUNG READERS

One snowy morning...

two friends found the oddest things
stuck in a giant pile of snow.

They wondered what all the stuff was for—

then they figured it out!

It took one lumpy kickball,
part of a wooden leg...

and a lot of know-how...

to cook a pot of
dragon tooth soup.

The tall rowboat—
turned upside down—
was a perfect table.

The grand curtain made a lovely tablecloth.

The gold anchor was
a neat candleholder.

The six small shields were very pretty plates.

And the pair of fish puppets? Well, they were...

Amazing hats!

The party was a big success.

But afterward, the two friends wondered: what if someone else had been planning to have a dragon-tooth-soup party?

So the very next morning...

they returned almost everything...

to about the same place.

*For those who have helped me to see things differently:*
*Kimm, Chloë, and Erwin*

**K.T.**


**For Gray**

**D.W.**

DIAL BOOKS FOR YOUNG READERS
An imprint of Penguin Random House LLC, New York

Text copyright © 2019 by Kevin Tseng
Illustrations copyright © 2019 by Dana Wulfekotte

Visit us at penguinrandomhouse.com

ISBN 9780735230415 · Printed in China · 10 9 8 7 6 5 4 3 2 1

Designed by Jason Henry · Text set in Chianti
The artwork for this book was created with pencil and colored digitally.